our
generation®

This is Evelyn's story.

EVELYN™

IN THE LIMELIGHT

BY

JULIE DRISCOLL

ILLUSTRATED BY TRISH ROUELLE

An Our Generation® *book*

MAISON JOSEPH BATTAT LTD. *Publisher*

A very special thanks to the editor,
Joanne Burke Casey.

Our Generation® Books is a registered trademark of Maison Joseph Battat Ltd.
Text copyright © 2011 by Julie Driscoll
ISBN: 978-0-9844904-3-1
Printed in China

For Mr. Deschenes and Sue McKay

Read all the adventures in the
Our Generation® Book Series

One Smart Cookie
featuring Hally™

Blizzard on Moose Mountain
featuring Katelyn™

Stars in Your Eyes
featuring Sydney Lee™

The Note in the Piano
featuring Mary Lyn™

The Mystery of the Vanishing Coin
featuring Eva®

Adventures at Shelby Stables
featuring Lily Anna®

The Sweet Shoppe Mystery
featuring Jenny™

The Jumpstart Squad
featuring Juliet™

The Dress in the Window
featuring Audrey-Ann™

The Jukebox Babysitters
featuring Ashley-Rose™

In the Limelight
featuring Evelyn™

CONTENTS

Chapter One   A Dinosaur Ate My Homework   Page 9

Chapter Two   First Rehearsal   Page 17

Chapter Three   A Bedtime Story   Page 24

Chapter Four   Bending the Rules   Page 31

Chapter Five   Getting Into Character   Page 41

Chapter Six   Longing to Be Different   Page 47

Chapter Seven   Just a Frog on a Log   Page 57

Chapter Eight   Friendship   Page 65

Chapter Nine   Opening Night   Page 73

Chapter Ten   Being Me   Page 87

EXTRA! EXTRA! READ ALL ABOUT IT!
Big words, wacky words, powerful words, funny words...
what do they all mean? They are marked with this symbol *.
Look them up in the Glossary at the end of this book.

Chapter One

A DINOSAUR ATE MY HOMEWORK

I was a bundle of nerves as I headed up the steps of the Gardner School. Part of me was excited to learn the "big" news but another part of me was afraid.

My little sister Lucille and her friend Rory trailed a few feet behind me. They were giggling and talking silly stuff—something to do with the clay dinosaurs they'd made and how Lucille's had an extremely small head, stripes like a zebra and a tail like a bunny. She named it Hoppozorious and it quickly became the family pet we'd never had.

Whatever though! I had much bigger concerns. Today would be the day I'd find out whether or not I got the lead role of Iris in the school play. I thought my chances were pretty good but there was always Grace. She's my strongest competition.

Grace is older than I am—a sixth grader. And she's more experienced, having already gotten a few important roles.

When she was only a fourth grader she played a white cat in the show *Nine Hundred Lives*. I was the baker. We each had speaking lines and a solo* but Grace had way more lines than I did. Those are the types of roles that are usually given to the older kids with more experience. But people often comment that Grace and I have natural talent and our director, Mr. Deschenes, notices that.

Grace had also taken some time off last year to try other afterschool activities. There isn't anything wrong with that, but I'd put my time in. Not because I felt I had to, but because I wanted to.

I'd been patiently waiting for the perfect role and it had finally arrived.

In the play *Once Upon an Elf*, the lead character, Iris, is a young Asian girl who is required to act and dress like all the other girls in her village and this makes her unhappy. She longs for a life with fewer rules and responsibilities—a life where she can just be herself and spend more time doing the things she enjoys, like playing in her grandfather's garden or swimming in the nearby pond. And that's exactly how I feel!

During my dull, boring school year, going to drama club where I can act, sing, dance and be up onstage in the

10

limelight*, is the one thing that I really look forward to. I wish I could be a performer all day, every day. Seriously though! It's bad enough that I have to suffer through the same old routine, day after day, week after week: school, lunch, recess and then home to do even more schoolwork, eat dinner, brush my teeth and go to bed. *Boring!*

At least when I'm at drama club I can express myself. I can dress up in fancy costumes and be *different*. When I'm at school I'm exactly the same as all the other girls. We all look the same in our uniforms and, like sheep in a herd, we move from one place to the next doing the same old *boring* thing.

My best friend Kiley was waiting for me outside my locker. She crossed her fingers and smiled. As I got closer her smile faded a bit. "Why are your eyes all…red-like?" she asked.

"Don't worry about it," I said.

I'd been so nervous about getting the part of Iris that I had cried about it the entire night before—so much so that my eyes were all puffy and swollen. My dad told me to quit being such a drama queen. But that's who I am. It's both a blessing and a curse.

Kiley was also nervous because she was going to learn whether or not she got the job of assistant stage manager. Kiley enjoys working behind the scenes as part of the "crew." They work on set design, stage lighting and sound. And the stage manager and assistant stage manager oversee everything that is "crew" related. It's a perfect fit for Kiley because she's not only artistic but a little shy, too.

Kiley is her happiest when she's designing, painting or working those spotlights so they're all pointed in the right direction onstage. And I'm happiest when I'm up onstage with all those spotlights pointed directly at *me*.

"Evelyn!" My teacher, Mrs. Power, interrupted my thoughts. She held out her hand. "May I have your science homework please?"

I'd been so distracted that I didn't even remember walking with Kiley to our classroom and sitting down at my desk. I pulled my homework assignment from my folder.

"What happened?" asked Mrs. Power, examining the spectacle* that I'd handed to her. The paper was all crinkly and a large chunk was missing from its right corner.

"Um...a dinosaur...not a real dinosaur...but this clay thing that my sister made...well it was *sorta kinda* hungry and my sister said it liked homework so I gave it a corner that wasn't being used."

"And how did your assignment get so wrinkled?" my teacher asked me.

"Lucille's dinosaur is a Hoppozorious and it hops, so..."

"Never mind," she interrupted. Then she moved on.

My classmates giggled and the rest of the day was one big blur.

When the last school bell finally rang, Kiley and I met at our lockers. We grabbed our backpacks and scurried down a long hallway, past the school cafeteria. We crossed from the main building into the drama wing* by way of an indoor bridge. A painting of a man, along with a gold plaque that read, "The Albert A. Rose Wing," hung on a wall at the entranceway to the wing.

Albert Rose was a man who had donated a ton of money to the Gardner School so that a drama wing could be built. I know the story inside and out because each year, at the start of a new play, Mr. Deschenes (we call him Mr. D for short) gives us all a speech about the history of the Gardner School and how a generous man named Mr. Rose, who was extremely passionate* about the theater, wanted to ensure that other children could have the same opportunities that he'd had. Mr. D usually ends his speech by telling us that we should all display our gratitude by working hard to be not only good, but great.

Two pieces of paper, one for cast members and the other for crew, were tacked up on the auditorium doors. A crowd of students had already formed in front of them. Kiley easily made her way over to the crew list. A few seconds later she was back at my side, whispering in my ear, "I got it! I'm the new assistant stage manager!" She was all smiles, yet still quietly trying not to draw attention to herself.

"That's great Kiley," I said. I was happy for her but selfishly more concerned with learning *my* fate at that particular moment.

As students moved away from the list I studied their faces for clues. One girl, Linda, smiled at me. I couldn't tell if it was a "congratulations" smile or an "I feel sorry for you" smile. Then I spotted Grace. She was directly in front of me, checking the list with her friend. They both shrieked loudly, then hugged.

My heart sank. I no longer wanted to see the list. Grace's excitement could only mean one thing. But there was nowhere to go except forward as the kids behind me steered me toward the piece of paper.

The names were listed in alphabetical order. I located K for Kneeland, then Evelyn. I followed the dotted lines with my finger over to the right. My heart was pounding a mile a minute as I read the cast name assigned to me... *Iris*.

I double-checked. And sure enough—my name, Evelyn Kneeland, on the left matched up perfectly with the name Iris, on the right.

I got it! I got the lead role!

Chapter Two

FIRST REHEARSAL

"Butterflies and bees over here, dragonflies and fish over there!"

The first rehearsal was always a bit crazy and unorganized.

Mr. D had just given the Albert A. Rose speech on greatness and we were now breaking up into groups to go over the script* and read our lines.

The students who didn't have big speaking roles, like my friends Nancy and Leah, and Lucille's friend Rory, were led off to a corner of the stage by Ms. Damiano, the choreographer*. They were going to begin learning dance steps.

Kiley was up on stage as well, looking official with her headset and notebook. She was speaking to Buckley, an eighth grader, and also the stage manager for the past two years.

The other cast members and I sat on the floor in front of

the stage and read through the script while Mr. D took notes.

Finally, after about an hour, Mr. D called a break. Everyone jumped up and rushed to the back of the auditorium toward the break room.

The break room was a cool little lounge equipped with a refrigerator, TV, CD player and even a foosball table. I loved going there and hanging out with everyone. Sometimes on a Friday night we'd all stay late, order pizza and rehearse our lines. But it never felt like work, especially because most of the drama kids were my friends.

I spotted Kiley exiting the auditorium and heading toward the break room. I hurried to catch up to her. Suddenly I heard my name being called.

"Evelyn. You need to come with me for your first fitting!"

It was Mrs. McKay. She's the official costume designer for all the Gardner School plays. Mrs. McKay has been with the drama program since as long as I can remember and she's created the most beautiful costumes. I was a little disappointed that I couldn't go to the break room but I was also excited to see what my costume looked like.

As I turned and re-entered the auditorium I noticed an elderly man speaking to Mr. D. He wore a bright red scarf around his neck, which is probably why I noticed him in the first place. I dashed down the aisle toward the stage.

"Congratulations Evelyn. You must be very excited," Mrs. McKay said as I followed her backstage and down the hallway toward the costume room.

"Thanks!" I replied. "I am."

I'd been hearing the word "congratulations" a lot that day and I had my responses down cold*. "Thanks," and "Yes, I know, it's great!"

Even Grace congratulated me. She'd gotten the role of Fuchsia, a flower fairy who befriends Iris. I thought she'd be upset because she didn't get the lead but she told me that she didn't want such a big part because it was way too much responsibility. "When I was the white cat," said Grace, "I had so many lines I was afraid I wasn't going to remember them. Plus, I still get a little nervous up on stage. Fuchsia is the perfect part for me."

Not as many kids congratulated Kiley for getting the assistant stage manager role, but she didn't seem to mind.

When we arrived at the costume room, Mrs. McKay pointed to a sketch of an Asian girl tacked up on her bulletin board.

"That's what you'll wear for the opening act," she said. The girl in the sketch wore a red kimono* with a white sash and trim and matching slippers. She was holding a parasol in one hand and a fan in the other and wore her hair up in a high bun with two stick-like things coming out of it.

Mrs. McKay measured my waist, arms and legs. Then she opened a large trunk and shuffled through it, pulling out a parasol and a fan similar to the ones in the sketch. "Keep these in your dressing room and don't lose them," she said.

"I won't," I promised.

Dressing room! I suddenly remembered something important. I had a lead role. That meant that I got my very own dressing room with my very own star on

21

the door with *my* name on it. I'd been so used to sharing a dressing room with all the other female cast members—I'd been so used to my star being just another star on a door—another sparkle in the sky as I used to say.

Mrs. McKay stopped me before I could sprint off. "Hold on." She sifted through a small bin marked "hair accessories" and pulled out two long sticks. "These go in your hair. They're hair sticks. And take these, too." She handed me a pair of red slippers.

"Thanks!" I said. Then I dashed out the door and down the hallway.

I passed the first dressing room that I used to have to share with everyone else. A bunch of gold stars with the cast members' names on them were already taped to the door. *Poor little sparkles,* I thought, *having to share a dressing room.*

I arrived at the next door. There it was—my name on a gold star—all by itself, hanging on my very own dressing room door. I turned the knob and entered. It was a spacious* room with a dressing table and mirror at the far wall, a clothes rack with a few hangers on it, a worn-out sofa and a costume trunk just like the one in the costume room.

I sat at the dressing table, undid my ponytail and twisted it into a high bun. Then I placed the two hair sticks in it. I'd barely been able to admire myself and enjoy my new hangout when a voice called out over the loudspeaker.

"Evelyn Kneeland, you're needed onstage!"

It was Mr. D calling me. I jumped up from my chair and hurried back down the hallway. I suddenly got the feeling that being a star in a play and not just a sparkle on a door was going to be a lot more work than I thought.

Chapter Three

A BEDTIME STORY

I tiptoed into the bedroom, trying not to wake Lucille. A teddy bear nightlight, required by Lucille because she was afraid of monsters, made it easy for me to see where I was going. But the floor near my bed was still a little dark and I trampled something cold and squishy with my bare feet. I picked it up and quickly established* that it was a piece of clay—probably from Lucille's dinosaur.

It had been a long week and I was glad the weekend had finally arrived. I'd stayed later than usual to rehearse my lines and have pizza with a few of the other cast members and for once, I was looking forward to bedtime. Suddenly the light clicked on.

"Look Evelyn." My little sister pulled a small, strange looking object from under her covers. It looked like a creature from outer space. "I made a friend for Hoppozorious. Her name is Yippie."

"Isn't dinosaur week over?" I asked.

"It's over in a month because it's dinosaur *month*, not week," said Lucille. "She's from the pterosaur group. They're one of the smaller dinosaurs. I imagine they used to make yipping sounds when they called out to one another. Wait!" Lucille quickly searched her covers. "She lost her tail!"

"Here." I handed Lucille the flattened piece of clay that I'd placed on my nightstand.

She took the mangled* tail that I'd stepped on and reattached it to her friend, Yippie.

I pulled the two sticks from my hair.

"What are those?" asked Lucille.

"They're my hair accessories that I wear in the first act."

"They look like plain old sticks. Why do you need to wear those?"

"They're part of my costume. I also have red slippers, a fan and a parasol. See?" I pointed to the objects lying beside my backpack in my "messy corner" of our bedroom. I knew I wasn't supposed to bring them home but I was *sorta kinda* planning on wearing a few of the items to school the following Monday.

"What's the story about?" asked Lucille.

I knew most of the beginning of the story by heart because I'd been studying my script all week with the other cast members. However, I decided it would make more sense if I told Lucille a shortened version.

"It's about a young Asian girl named Iris who was tired of the same old boring routine day after day: tutoring, lunch, afternoon tea with all the other girls in her village, dinner, chores and finally, bedtime."

"That doesn't sound *too* bad," said Lucille.

"No, I guess not, but Iris wished she had more time to play in the garden or swim in the pond. However, rules and schedules kept her from doing what she liked to do. As part of her daily routine, Iris was required to attend afternoon tea with all the other girls in the village so that she could learn proper etiquette."

"What's that?"

"It's a bunch of rules or suggestions on the proper way of doing things like minding your manners and all that stuff."

"Oh."

"During afternoon tea, she was expected to sit up straight, sip slowly from a porcelain* cup and be extra careful not to make any clanking noises with her spoon. And when she was out walking she had to shield her face from the sun using a parasol."

"Why?" Lucille asked.

"I don't know. It's just another rule she had to follow, I guess. But she was mostly bothered by the fact that she was required to dress the same as all the other girls in the village so she wouldn't stand out and be 'different.' She complained that it made her feel like just another leaf on a vine.

"Anyhow," I continued, "playing in her grandfather's

27

garden or swimming in the nearby pond were her favorite things to do. Her grandfather's garden was filled with beautiful flowering plants and shrubs. When she played in the garden she could sing and dance and make as much noise as she wanted without offending anyone. And when she swam in the pond she could splash about and just be herself.

"There was one flowering shrub in the garden that Iris admired most—a beautiful orchid plant, covered with the prettiest rosy pink flowers. It was her grandfather's favorite as well. He nurtured* and tended to it with extra care and affection, and it showed.

"One afternoon, on her way to tea, Iris stopped at the garden entrance and peeked inside. The orchids were in full bloom and as she admired them from afar she felt as though they were calling out to her to come closer. So she did.

"She stood up close to the pretty pink orchids, marveling* at their beauty and breathing in their perfumed scent when she suddenly had an idea. *What harm would it be,* she thought, *if I were to pick just one orchid to wear as a decoration in my hair.* She saw it as an opportunity to feel special for a change; to be 'different.'

"She plucked one of the orchids from the flowering shrub, placed it behind her ear and hurried off to afternoon tea.

"During tea, all the girls from the village admired Iris and the beautiful orchid she wore. The extra attention she received made her feel special and pretty.

"Soon, many of the village girls decided that, like Iris, they wanted to feel special, too. So one by one, they snuck into her grandfather's garden and plucked a pink flower from the orchid plant.

"The following day, almost all the village girls were wearing orchids behind their ears. Iris was no longer 'different,' and she suddenly felt like just another flower in a garden.

"Iris's grandfather became very angry when he realized what had happened. All that remained of his beautiful orchid plant was a bunch of green leaves and a few broken stems."

"Did she get in trouble?" Lucille asked.

"Yes she did," I replied. "As punishment, Iris's grandfather sent her to the garden and made her sit on a bench and think about what she had done."

"Then what?" asked Lucille.

"We should stop here," I said. "I'm getting really sleepy."

"Fine," agreed Lucille. But she made me pinky swear with Hoppozorius and Yippie as witnesses that I'd tell her the rest of the story the following night.

"We have three months before the play," I told her. "That's plenty of time to get through the story."

Lucille agreed. She adjusted her dinosaurs on her pillow and covered them with a small blanket.

Then we closed our eyes and drifted off to sleep.

Chapter Four

BENDING THE RULES

Lucille knew all about my plan at the bus stop the following Monday when I swapped out my boring school shoes with the red slippers from my backpack and then placed the sticks in my hair.

She had been telling me all weekend that I wasn't going to get away with it. Then, as we were boarding the bus, she said that I was going to "stick" out like a sore thumb.

I didn't believe her though. I felt pretty confident that no one would notice. *What's the harm in being a little "different"?* I thought.

But sure enough, I hadn't even gotten a few feet from the school when I saw Mrs. McReynolds standing at the entranceway greeting all the students. Mrs. McReynolds is our school principal and she's the strictest, most rule-making person

I've ever known. She noticed me right away.

"Evelyn, would you go to my office and wait for me there?" she asked.

It didn't sound like a question though. It sounded more like a command with a question mark at the end of it. Of course I said yes, and off I went to Mrs. McReynolds' office.

When Mrs. McReynolds arrived she sat down behind her desk and began with another question that I had a feeling she already knew the answer to.

"Did you lose your school shoes?"

"No," I replied. "I just felt like wearing something different today."

"You do understand the school uniform policy, don't you? And you've read through the student handbook with your parents, haven't you?" Two more questions.

"Yes, but it's only shoes and a few sticks sticking out of my hair…I didn't think anyone would mind."

She went on to give me a lecture about school policy and dress code and told me that whether I liked it or not, I was required to follow the rules.

There was another student waiting outside Mrs. McReynolds' office. I could see through the glass window that it was Liam, a fifth-grade boy in my drama club. Liam got a role as a fish in the play and based on the look of him, I had a feeling he was going to get in a lot more trouble than I was.

Mrs. McReynolds hurried our meeting along. She made me switch back into my school shoes and remove the sticks. Then she wrapped up our discussion by telling me that I needed to follow the rules and that the sticks were part of a costume and not part of my school uniform and that someone could get hurt and did I understand what she was trying to say to me.

"Yes. Yes. Yes." I nodded so much that I felt like a bobblehead.

As she handed me a hall pass, she reminded me that hat day was the following day and I'd be able to accessorize my hair however I saw fit.

I'd been so wrapped up in all the drama stuff that I'd forgotten all about hat day.

Each month our school assigns one "dress-up"

day where students can express themselves by adding something special or fun to their uniforms. On hat days students are allowed to wear a hat or accessory on their head. There are other dress-up days as well, such as funky shoe day and team spirit day. But hat day is my favorite.

At least I have that to look forward to, I thought.

I walked out of Mrs. McReynolds' office. Liam had colored his face with orange marker and lined his eyes and lips in black. I shook my head at him and hurried off to class.

చి చి

Drama club was busy as usual. I missed break time again because Mrs. McKay needed to fit me for my fairy costume. It was yellow and pink with green wings and a skirt that looked like it was made out of flower petals. She pinned the waist and then adjusted the flower petals at the hemline*.

Come to think of it, I'd only been to the break room once since rehearsals had begun. I missed that part a little but I also decided that getting a lead role was a good trade-off. Most of the time I took a quick break in my dressing room. I loved the fact that I had my very own dressing room. It made me feel important.

While Mrs. McKay tightened the back of my fairy dress I noticed sketches of the bee and fish costumes hanging on her bulletin board. She had numbers associated with them, "15 bees" and "12 fish." Many of my friends at our lunch table were bees like Theresa, Darah and Sydney. And some of the boys in my class were fish like Liam. I felt a little sorry for them because their costumes were all the same—not different like mine.

"Here's the wand that goes with your fairy costume," said Mrs. McKay, handing it to me. She told me to store it in the costume trunk in my dressing room.

Afterward, I went to my dressing room to drop off my wand and have a snack. I sat on the sofa and glanced around. *How great to have my very own hangout,* I thought to myself.

I walked over to the trunk and was about to put the wand inside when I suddenly changed my mind. *What harm would it be if I brought it home just for one day?* I thought. I wanted to show it to Lucille. So, I slipped the wand into my backpack and hurried back to rehearsal.

As I rounded the corner to the stage, Kiley jumped out from behind a curtain and startled me. She grabbed my arm. "Come with me. I need to show you something."

She led me to the far right side of the stage. "Wait here!" she commanded.

She disappeared behind one of the backdrops and reappeared pushing a large contraption*. It was a huge green wooden structure resting on a dolly* and painted to look like a giant shrub.

"This is going to be the orchid plant in the flower garden," she explained.

"But where are all the flowers?" I asked.

"They're over here." Kiley led me to a box in the back corner. Inside it were tons of pretty paper flowers crafted to look like orchids.

I took one from the box and inspected it. The rosy pink flowers were almost the size of softballs. "They're beautiful! Where'd you get them?"

"I made them. I worked all weekend on them and they're finally done. The stems go into these holes here." She pointed out the tiny little holes that were scattered throughout the green structure.

"Why are the flowers so big?" I asked.

"Mr. D wants to make sure that everyone can see them from the audience," Kiley replied.

I took a paper flower and placed it behind my ear. "Can I have this one?" I asked. "It will help me to get into character." I also secretly liked the fact that, like Iris, it made me appear different from everyone else.

Kiley agreed, and for the rest of rehearsal, all the other cast members admired the decorative flower accessory behind my ear.

When rehearsal was over I skipped out of the auditorium, feeling especially pretty. A sorta familiar looking person was there, sitting at the back of the auditorium. It was the elderly man with the red scarf. I was so busy wondering who he was that I wasn't paying attention to where I was going. I stumbled into a box of crew supplies and my backpack and I went flying into the aisle.

From where I was lying I could see Liam standing over me. There were still traces of orange and black marker on his face but it was now mixed in with red as though he had scrubbed his face way too hard in an attempt to get it off. I sat up and started to collect my stuff. Liam helped a little by kicking a few books in my direction.

In some ways Liam was a lot like me—always trying to be different and stand out from the crowd. He also had some talent when it came to singing and acting but when he wasn't up onstage he was usually way too much of a goof-off.

I located my paper orchid and placed it back behind my ear. "Who is that guy?" I asked Liam.

"I don't know," he replied, as he stepped over my backpack and headed toward the exit. "He's just a guy I guess."

The man was leafing through a large document and even though he was sitting about ten seats away I could smell his cologne from where I was standing.

I gathered up the rest of my stuff and headed out the door.

Chapter Five

GETTING INTO CHARACTER

It had been another long day. Lucille and her clay friends were waiting patiently for me to come to bed so that they could hear more of the story.

"What happened to your sticks?" Lucille asked me as I rifled* through my backpack looking for my script.

"Oh, those. They *sorta kinda* got taken away."

"I told you, you shouldn't have done that," said Lucille.

"I know, but look what I have instead." I turned my head and leaned into the nightlight so that Lucille could see the paper flower behind my ear.

"Where'd you get that?" she asked.

"Kiley made a whole bunch of them. It helps me to get into character. I'm going to wear it for hat day tomorrow."

"What does getting into character mean?" my sister asked.

"It means it helps me to become the person I'm pretending to be so the audience members will believe me when I'm performing up onstage. Oh, and I almost forgot…" I did another search of my backpack, looking for the fairy wand. But it wasn't there. "Never mind," I told Lucille, as I climbed into bed. "I was going to show you my fairy wand but I must have left it in my dressing room."

I propped myself up on my pillow and grabbed a flashlight from my nightstand.

"Wow!" said Lucille, noticing the large document on my lap. "Is that the entire play?"

"Yes," I said shining the flashlight on it. "I have a lot of lines to memorize. Where did we leave off?"

"Umm, Iris got a time-out in the garden," said Lucille.

I located that page in the script and suddenly realized that it was one of the scenes where I'd be up onstage all by myself, wearing my kimono costume and singing a solo in front of hundreds of people. I got the chills just thinking about it.

"OK," I began. "Iris was sitting in the garden, sobbing uncontrollably and feeling sorry for herself. I sing a song here," I told her. "It's called 'Being Me.'

"All of a sudden Iris heard a strange sound. Startled, she looked around but didn't see anything.

"An unusual voice called out to her from somewhere in the

brush, 'You must stop crying at once!'

"She scanned her surroundings and there, on a low-lying branch of a nearby cherry blossom tree, Iris spotted a teeny, tiny elf, no more than a foot tall.

"'Who are you?' asked Iris.

"'Umm, *hello*! I'm an elf,' he said, as though Iris should have already known that. 'All your crying and carrying on is upsetting the flowers. What could be so awful that you should have to carry on like this for hours upon end?' he asked in his peculiar tone.

"Iris was a little confused by the elf's presence but went on to explain what had happened. Then she sobbed again as she told the elf how she was tired of following so many rules and that she wished she had more freedom to be different and do the things she loved to do.

"'Please,' the elf begged. 'No more crying. I told you it upsets the flowers and causes them to wilt.'

"Iris glanced around the garden. Some of the crocuses had begun to close their petals and the bluebells were bent forward with their tiny filaments* facing toward the ground.

"Iris wiped her eyes and tried to compose* herself while the elf hopped off the branch and settled on the grass in front of her. He began talking to himself. 'Hmm…yes…perhaps…that might work….' The elf was deep in thought.

"'I think I know a way I can help you,' he finally said.

"'How?' Iris asked.

"'It just so happens that Daisy Clove, the garden fairy who used to oversee this garden, up and left today. I'm in search of her replacement. All I need to do is say a few magic words and *poof*, you'd be a tiny fairy *and* this entire garden would be yours.'

"'What does a garden fairy do?' Iris asked.

"'A garden fairy dances and sings all day—from morning 'til dusk—entertaining the flowers.'

"'Fairies sing and dance for flowers?' she asked.

"'Like people, flowers enjoy being entertained, too. That's what makes them so beautiful. That's what helps them to grow and thrive*.'

"'So, that's it? Dance and sing all day? That's the only job of a garden fairy?'

"'Yup. Sing, dance and…oh yes, I almost forgot….' He handed Iris a fairy wand. 'The previous garden fairy left this behind. It contains fairy dust. Sprinkle each flower with fairy

44

dust as you go. It's the same as sending lots of hugs and kisses. If you do these things the result will be a beautiful, happy garden. And no crying allowed!' he exclaimed.

"'That sounds easy and fun,' said Iris.

"'Yes, however there is *one more* rule.' Then the elf went on to explain that under no condition can a garden fairy get her wings wet. 'On rainy days, you must wrap yourself inside a flower petal until the rain stops.'

"'Why?' Iris was curious.

"'A garden fairy with wet wings cannot fly. It takes days and days for a garden fairy's wings to dry.'

"Iris thought for a moment. *Just the two rules? No crying and no getting my wings wet? How hard could that be? I'm used to following many, many rules.*

"She glanced around the garden which was filled with budding flowers set among charming little stepping stones, a trickling fountain and some cherry blossom trees. *What a fun job being a garden fairy would be,* she thought. So Iris begged the elf to turn her into a garden fairy.

"*Poppyseed, Juniper, Polites, Fern—Magisto, Swallowtail, Pixie and Stern—Oscillate, Pivot, Metamorphose, Transcend—*

to a spritely young fairy in the end!'

"The elf said a few magical words and *poof*! Iris was quickly transformed into a tiny fairy, no bigger than a fruit fly."

I looked over at Lucille. Her eyes were beginning to close. Yippie and Hoppozorious had toppled onto their sides and Yippie's tail had fallen off again.

I turned off my flashlight then flung my script toward my messy corner. Lucille didn't hear the clatter it made when it missed and landed near the trash barrel because she was already sound asleep.

I wasn't far behind.

46

Chapter Six

LONGING TO BE DIFFERENT

The following night Lucille was waiting up for me, but I'd had an awful day and didn't feel like telling the story. She was perched up in her bed, surrounded by some of her favorite stuffed animals and dinosaur friends. And she was still wearing her silly hat from hat day. It was a tall furry top hat with red and green polka dots and a few antennae sticking out of the top.

I was fairly certain that no one else had looked like Lucille today—and that was part of my problem. It seemed that most of the girls in my class had gotten the same idea as I had for hat day and decided to wear flowers behind their ears, too.

When I arrived at school I noticed it right away. With the exception of a few classmates, like Kiley, who wore a striped headband, and Lisa, who had on a colorful scarf, most of the female students in our class were wearing flowers behind their ears. Some girls wore silk flowers in their hair, others had made their own paper flowers and some girls actually had on *real* flowers. But worst of all— many of the girls from drama club had gotten their flowers from Kiley's box.

Of course, Liam had no trouble standing out from the crowd. He'd taken one of the fish head costumes from the costume room. It was a large, stuffed goldfish head that made him appear about two feet taller. We could all see him coming down the hallway from a mile away.

I had a feeling he was going to get in trouble for taking one of the drama costumes and sure enough, moments later, I watched as the big fish head bobbed behind a taller Mrs. McReynolds, down the hallway toward her office.

At lunchtime Kiley became very upset when she noticed all the drama club girls at our table wearing the flowers she'd made. She left the lunch table immediately. And she wasn't at rehearsal later that day.

I didn't think that things could get any worse, but they did. At rehearsal, Mr. D asked me to grab my wand so that I could practice with it in a few of the scenes. I searched my dressing room and backpack again but it was nowhere to be found. Then when it was time to go over lines I couldn't find my script.

Mr. D and Mrs. McKay were disappointed in me. Mrs. McKay informed me that if I didn't locate the wand she'd have to order a new one and I'd have to pay for it. Mr. D told me that when he assigned me a lead role, part of the reason was because he thought I would act responsibly. I felt as though I'd let them both down.

At bedtime I searched through the pile of stuff in my messy corner again, hoping the fairy wand would magically appear. But it didn't. I couldn't imagine where I'd left it. I spotted my script near the trash barrel. I grabbed it and climbed into bed.

"Did the flower help you get into character?" Lucille asked me.

I'd almost forgotten I was wearing it. "*Sorta…kinda…I guess so,*" I sighed as I removed the paper orchid and placed it on my nightstand.

I glanced over at Lucille and, despite my bad day, I couldn't help but smile. She was completely unaware of her unusual display. Between her crazy hat, her bizarre-looking dinosaurs and all her colorful stuffed animals, Lucille's bed looked like something right out of a circus act.

Knowing that she was eager for a bedtime story, I asked the question anyway. "Do I have to tell you the story tonight?"

"Yes!" she said expectantly. "We were at the part where Iris got turned into a garden fairy."

"Fine," I sighed. I grabbed my flashlight and flipped

to the correct page in the script. It was hard to say no to Lucille. She was always so upbeat. I never wanted to disappoint her.

"OK, so at first, Iris really enjoyed being a fairy," I said. "Singing and dancing from dawn 'til dusk felt more like play than work. She bounced from one flower to the next singing softly to them and sending them all hugs and kisses with her fairy wand.

"The bees and butterflies also worked busily in the garden as a team—doing their jobs as nature intended. The humming noise that the bees made had a calming effect on the flowers. They produced honey for their queen and spread pollen throughout the garden so that additional flowers could grow. And the butterflies were like fluttering works of art, contributing* to the overall beauty of the garden while also assisting the bees with pollination*.

"Iris liked the fact that she was the only fairy in the garden. It made her feel special. But the garden was big and filled with lots of beautiful flowers so it took her all day to visit each and every one. By the end of the day she was so exhausted that she'd curl up in a flower petal and fall fast asleep.

"After a few weeks Iris realized that being a garden fairy wasn't all it was cracked up to be. Singing and dancing all day, every day, was beginning to feel more like work than play.

"One sunny afternoon, while tending to several orange trumpet flowers which had grown like weeds stretching all the way up to the top of the garden wall, Iris stopped to catch her breath. Tired and thirsty, she sat on the wall, fanning herself with a tiny leaf bud. She gazed over at the cool, refreshing pond that she used to enjoy swimming in as a girl. Just then, a tiny fairy flitted past her.

"Iris was happy to see someone similar to her. She called to the fairy, 'Where are you going?'

"The fairy turned and flew back toward the garden wall where Iris was sitting. 'Hello! My name is Fuchsia. I'm on my way to the pond. Sometimes I go there to take a little break and dip my toes in the cool water. Come with me,' she said.

"Happily, Iris jumped up and flew over to the pond with the fairy."

I paused for a second. "Grace plays the part of Fuchsia," I told Lucille. "We both sing and dance together in this scene. Her fairy dress is similar to mine except it's pink and maroon."

"That sounds nice. Then what happens?" Lucille asked.

"The two fairies sat along the shady edge of the pond, dipping their toes in the water and exchanging flower stories. Fuchsia explained that she was a wildflower fairy in charge of a field close by. She also told Iris that she had been friends with Daisy Clove, the previous garden fairy.

"'Why did she leave?' Iris asked curiously.

"'A bunch of village girls destroyed a beautiful orchid plant in her garden. That made Daisy Clove very angry and she just up and left.'

"'Oh, I see,' said Iris, not wanting to let on that she'd had something to do with that.

"As they sat by the water's edge, Iris spotted a lotus flower in the center of the pond. And although pond flowers were not part of her domain* she decided that she wanted to visit it and send it hugs and kisses with her fairy wand.

"Fuchsia warned her not to go. She told Iris that she was taking a big chance and that she could get her wings wet. 'That's the water fairies' job. They have special waterproof wings!' she exclaimed.

"But Iris felt confident that nothing would happen. Besides, it was such an unusual looking flower. She wanted to see it up close. So she spread her wings and flitted over to the lily pad.

"The lotus blossom was truly an amazing sight up close. It had many long, pale pink petals and an unusual yellow pod* in the center. She lifted her wand and sent tiny specks of fairy hugs and kisses to it.

"Just as Iris was about to head back, a large school of fish swam by. One of the fish jumped up out of the water and did a triple flip in the air. The splash that it made upon its return looked more like a tidal wave* from the perspective* of the tiny fairy on top of the lily pad. Water gushed over the lily pad and, not surprisingly, Iris got drenched.

"Iris's wings were heavily weighed down from being so soaked and she could hardly speak.

"Fuchsia flew over to Iris and hovered above the lily pad. 'I'll go find the elf. Perhaps he'll know what to do,' she said. 'In the meantime, don't go anywhere! Your wings are much too heavy to fly.' Then, shaking her head in disbelief, Fuchsia fluttered off toward the woods to locate the elf."

"Is my friend Rory in that scene?" Lucille interrupted.

"Yes, she's one of the fish that swims by," I told her. Then I described how Mr. D had rented a backdrop for the scene that contained a greenish-blue pond and flowing willow trees. It rolls down during a curtain change and makes me feel like I'm really sitting beside a pond.

I yawned. "Let's stop here," I told Lucille. "It's getting late."

"*Fine*," she said.

I hopped out of bed and placed the script in my backpack so I wouldn't forget it the next day. Then I crawled back under my covers.

Tomorrow's another day, I thought. *It can only get better*. I hoped that Kiley wasn't still upset with me and that I could somehow figure out a way to make it up to her.

Chapter Seven

JUST A FROG ON A LOG

Things didn't get much better in the days that followed. Kiley didn't wait for me at our lockers like she usually did. And she wasn't at our lunch table either.

At rehearsal she worked in the sound booth the entire time so I never got a chance to talk to her.

To make matters worse, I still hadn't located my fairy wand.

I was beginning to miss the days when I had fewer responsibilities and more free time. I also missed having a friend like Kiley to talk to.

When the weekend finally arrived again I was happy to be able to rest a little and get a break from my usual routine. Kiley and I would normally get together and go to the movies or hang out. Sometimes we'd pick out a craft project to work on together. She had tons of craft kits that had been given to her as gifts over the years, mainly because everyone knew that was something she liked to do.

But she had been avoiding me. And for the first

weekend in a long time, I was actually starting to feel a bit bored.

Of course, Lucille was happy to have my undivided attention. She begged me to tell her more of the story. I had nothing better to do so I agreed.

Lucille and I sat on my bed and continued where we'd left off.

"Iris sat on the lily pad and wept. With wings too heavy to fly, she had no other option but to wait for them to dry while Fuchsia went for help. The bees and butterflies were also upset with Iris. She'd left them in quite a situation. Now their work would be doubly hard.

"The beautiful lotus flower had started to wilt as a result of all her crying. And all the fish and dragonflies moved to the furthest section of the pond.

"A frog sat on a log that floated among the lily pads. It let out a giant RRRR-IIIBBBB-IITT!

"The deep, groaning sound startled Iris. 'Who are you?' she asked, frightened by the green, scaly skinned creature who appeared gigantic to her.

"The frog's big, bulgy eyes blinked as he spoke. 'I'm

just a frog, sitting on a log.' But then he corrected himself. 'Actually, I'm not *just* a frog, I'm a magical frog.'

"'A magical frog?' Iris asked.

"'Yes, I'm a frog and I also know magic so that would make me a magical frog, sitting on this here log!' he said a bit impatiently, as if she should have understood.

"Iris explained her predicament* to the frog and asked him if he could use his magical powers to turn her back into a young girl.

"'Sorry, no can do,' he said. 'My powers only work on things related to water. But, while I can't turn you back into a human, I could certainly turn you into a fish if you'd like. They're a happy bunch and they don't really have any responsibilities or rules to follow. All they do is swim aimlessly* about all day, enjoying each other's company and having fun.'

"Iris thought about the frog's proposition*. 'I do enjoy swimming…but I prefer to be different. I don't want to be just another fish in a pond.'

"Then the frog paused as he thought for a moment.

'Hmm…yes…I suppose so…that just might work…'

"'What?' asked Iris curiously.

"'Although they usually reside* in rivers or oceans I suppose a pond would work, too. I could turn you into a mermaid if you'd like.'

"'Why would I want to become a mermaid?' asked Iris.

"'For starters, mermaids are different from all the other water creatures. You'd be the only one in this pond,' said the frog.

"'What do mermaids do?' asked Iris.

"'Swim, lounge around, daydream to their hearts' content—basically not much! And on occasion, when the mood strikes, they like to play the flute.'

"'Flute?' asked Iris.

"'Yes, the flute is a common instrument used by mermaids. It provides a soothing sound for all the water-related creatures.'

"'Are there any rules?' asked Iris.

"'No rules whatsoever,' replied the frog.

"'That sounds good to me,' said Iris.

"So the frog recited a few magic words: 'Nelumbo, Flexion, Spiral, Transcend—Convergent, Salamander Aquatic, Amend—an enchanting young mermaid in the end!' And *poof*! Iris was transformed from a tiny garden fairy into a lovely mermaid."

I paused for a second. "You should see my mermaid costume," I told Lucille. "It's so pretty. I wish I could bring it home to show you. It's light purple on the top with a sea-blue skirt and fins at the bottom."

"Cool!" said Lucille. "Did Iris like being a mermaid?"

"At first she liked it a lot. The water was very refreshing and she was happy that there were no rules to follow and no responsibilities whatsoever. She also enjoyed the fact that she was different from all the rest of the water creatures.

"*Poor little fish,* she thought as she watched them swim by, *following each other around in their little schools, looking exactly the same and doing exactly the same thing. How boring that must be!*"

"Is that when Rory sings?" Lucille asked.

"Yes," I said. "Rory and the other fish run around

doing breaststrokes with their arms, as though they're swimming. They sing a song that goes something like:

Fish in the pond, just like fish in the sea, swimming about aimlessly.

"Then Rory jumps up and yells, 'I'm happy being just plain old me!'"

"She's so excited about being a fish and having her own speaking part," said Lucille. "Then what happens?"

"Well, Fuchsia returned with the elf only to find that Iris was no longer waiting for them on the lily pad because she'd been turned into a mermaid. So, the elf went off to find another replacement fairy for the garden and Fuchsia went back to tending to her wildflowers."

I paused. "We're almost at the end," I told Lucille. Then I put down the script. "You're going to have to wait for the performance to hear the rest."

"Why?" Lucille asked, disappointed.

"What fun would it be if you came to my play and you already knew the ending? You *are* coming, right?"

"Yes," she replied.

"Good! Now you'll have something to look forward to. Besides, it's only a few months away."

"But that seems like forever!" Lucille moaned.

"I know," I said. I felt the same exact way.

Chapter Eight
FRIENDSHIP

On Sunday morning I called Kiley. Her mom told me that she was at school working on the set.

"Mom! Dad!" I called out. "Can I please get a ride over to the school today?" I suddenly knew how I could make things better between Kiley and me.

"On a Sunday?" asked my dad. "What's there for you to do on a Sunday?"

"Lots," I replied. "Kiley is there."

My dad agreed to drive me. So I put on an old pair of jeans and a T-shirt, pulled my hair back in a ponytail and we headed out the door.

The side door leading to the auditorium was unlocked. My dad walked me inside. We could hear hammering and drilling as we rounded the back hallway toward the stage.

Mr. D and the entire crew were hard at work. I noticed a few of the kids up onstage stringing tiny lights on what appeared to be a gigantic weeping willow tree, made out of cardboard with long green paper streamers hanging down.

I said goodbye to my dad and rushed off to find

Kiley. I located her in one of the stage wings*. She was going over the prop list* with another crew member.

She looked surprised to see me. "What are you doing here?"

"I came to help," I replied. Then I paused. "Kiley, I'm sorry about what happened to the flowers. If you haven't already remade them, I'd like to do that for you."

Kiley's lip began to tremble. She was trying not to cry but her eyes became watery. "No one realizes how hard I work and I never get any credit for it," she said through her tears. "I don't even mind. But what I do mind is that everyone thinks they can take something without giving any consideration as to how hard I've worked."

"I know," I said. "I'm really sorry. If you show me where the paper is, I'll make more flowers for you. You won't have to do a thing."

"Are you sure you want to…." She wiped the tears from her eyes. I could tell that my being there was helping to make her feel better.

"I'm sure. None of this would have happened if it

hadn't been for me. It's the least I can do."

I put my arm around Kiley and she led me to the supply room where pink tissue paper and pipe cleaners were stored.

I hauled the box of paper and supplies to the front of the stage. We sat on the floor of the auditorium and Kiley showed me how to make the first one. It was fairly easy. I just needed to cut the paper into rectangles and then fold them like an accordion*. I twisted a pipe cleaner around the center and pulled it tight. Then I fluffed out all the folds to form a pretty flower.

As I sat there making the orchids I looked around and realized how much time and effort the crew had put into making the set not just good, but great.

Some of the backdrops for the scenes looked like something you'd see in a professional* play. Like Kiley, the crew members didn't need to be in the limelight to feel special or important. Seeing the results of all their hard work was enough for them.

An hour had passed and I'd already made tons of flowers. Kiley came over and sat down beside me. She grabbed a pipe cleaner and some paper and began helping me.

I looked up and noticed Mr. D leading the man in the red scarf around the stage. He was showing him all the props and backdrops.

"Who is that guy?" I asked Kiley.

"I don't know. But he's been here a lot the past few weeks."

Mr. D and the mysterious man walked down the side stairs of the stage toward us. Just then, Buckley called over to Mr. D with a question. So,

Mr. D excused himself for a moment.

The man approached us. "Hello," he said. "I recognize you two. You're the young girl who plays Iris," he said to me. "And you're the other talented one who's responsible for this beautiful set," he said, nodding to Kiley.

We both smiled. I was surprised at how observant he was. "I'm Evelyn," I said.

"And I'm Kiley."

"Keep up the good work. Oh, I almost forgot." He walked over to the front of the stage. He leaned down behind the piano and picked up something. "I'm guessing this belongs to you," he said when he returned. "I noticed it lying in the aisle last week after you left."

"Thanks!" I said as he handed me my fairy wand.

"Excuse me everyone." Mr. D stood onstage and made an announcement. "We need to test the lighting." He instructed Kiley to go to the booth at the back of the auditorium. Kiley took the headset that had been hanging around her neck, placed it on her head and ran up the aisle toward the back.

Then Mr. D gestured to the gentleman to have a seat for a moment.

From the booth Kiley dimmed the lights and communicated with Buckley through her headset.

Buckley called out, "Cue* stage lights!" And then, "Cue backdrop!"

The backdrop containing the pond scene came rolling down. The huge willow tree that the crew members had been working on earlier was wheeled out to the center of the stage. Two other crew members rolled out a large fake rock, made out of foam, that looked a lot heavier than it actually was.

"Wow!" I gasped. A soft blue light shone down on the pond in the beautiful backdrop. And tiny, sparkly lights were strung about the wispy willow tree. The scene looked like something right out of an enchanted forest.

Mr. D called over to me. "Evelyn, since you're here, can you go get into position onstage? We'll go with Scene Eight from your script when you're sitting at the water's edge."

I scurried up the side stairs of the stage and sat on the big rock. I knew the scene he was referring to. It was the one just before Liam, playing the fish, pops his head up from behind the big rock and startles me.

Once I was in position, Kiley adjusted the lighting and shined a greenish-blue spotlight directly on me.

When the auditorium lights came back on again the man stood up and clapped.

"You've all done a wonderful job on this set," he said as soon as we got back.

"Girls, I see you've both met Mr. Rose," Mr. D said as he approached the three of us.

Mr. Rose, I thought. That name sounded oddly familiar to me.

We both nodded. Then Mr. Rose said his goodbyes and walked with Mr. D toward the exit.

I looked over at Kiley to see if she was thinking what I was thinking. I was fairly certain that the man we'd just met was *the* Mr. Rose, the person responsible for the drama wing. But he looked different—much older than the dark-haired man in the painting.

Chapter Nine
OPENING NIGHT

The next few months consisted of lots of hard work and very little time for play. I spent all my free time rehearsing songs and memorizing my lines while Kiley continued to work on the set—making it the best one yet. We didn't mind though, because we knew the end result would be not only a good performance but a great one!

The big day finally arrived. It was opening night and I had the jitters like never before. I sat alone in my dressing room, putting on my makeup and adjusting my hair sticks. It was oh so very quiet, and I suddenly found myself wishing that I had someone else to talk to and share my nervousness with. I realized that being just another sparkle on a door had its advantages.

I opened my dressing room door and peeked out. Rory and a few other girls were in the hallway adjusting their fish costumes. "Why are you out here?" I asked them.

"Because it's too crowded in our dressing room," Rory said.

I headed down the hall and opened the door to the community dressing room. There was a lot of commotion* and all the girls were laughing and joking around while they helped each other with hair and makeup. Lisa stopped me at the doorway and asked me to zip up her dragonfly costume. I was happy to help.

I told Rory and her friends, and anyone else who was interested, that they could get ready in my dressing room if they wanted. Then I spent the remainder of my time hanging out with the other cast members in the community dressing room. It felt just like the old days.

It was minutes before the curtain was set to open. Backstage, crew members dressed in all black rushed around while the cast members practiced their lines and made last-minute touchups to their hair and makeup. I could feel everyone's excitement, including my own.

Two of the crew members, Ali and Darlene, stood around me adjusting my hair and kimono. Then Kiley came over and attached a wireless microphone to my ear.

Moments later, Mr. D walked onto the stage and whispered to all of us, "Curtains up in two minutes!" My legs suddenly began to feel all wobbly and jelly-like.

Kiley gave me a big hug and wished me luck. Seconds later, Buckley called out, "Places everyone!" All the cast and crew members got into position.

From the other side of the curtain, Mr. D spoke

to the audience and made a few announcements. I stood at the center of the stage, taking deep breaths. At that point, aside from Mr. D's voice, it was so quiet and still that you could have heard a pin drop.

Then I heard Buckley's voice echoing off a headset as he called out instructions to the other crew members.

"Cue sound!" The speakers around the auditorium made a buzzing noise as they thumped on.

"Cue music!" Suddenly, music from the small orchestra in front of the stage began to play.

"Curtains up!" The large velvet curtains swayed back and forth as they slid open.

"Cue stage lights!" Some of the smaller backdrop lights came on but I was still in the dark.

Then a seventh grader who plays the role of the narrator* spoke a few introductory* words to the audience. "Once upon a time, in a faraway village, there lived a young girl who was tired of the same old, same old...."

A few moments later, a bright spotlight shone down on me.

I stood there in the limelight and opened with the song called "Being Me."

Like a fish in the sea, or a buzzing bee, I'm tired of being just plain old me!

As the show progressed I started to feel more and more confident. All the cast and crew members worked together doing their part and waiting for their cues.

We got to the fairy scene that Grace and I were in together. She rushed by me onstage flapping her arms, acting the part of Fuchsia on her way to the pond. She was a little nervous when she spoke her lines but she got through it OK. And when she sang her solo she was flawless*.

At some point, one of the petals on my fairy costume had come loose and was hanging off the back of my dress. Kiley noticed it right away from the booth and communicated the problem to Ali and Darlene. At the next scene change, they were right there with pins, adjusting the petal so it was perfect again.

When the curtain reopened, no one was the wiser* about what had gone on behind the scenes.

During intermission I peeked out from behind the curtain and spotted my mom, dad and Lucille sitting in the audience. Hoppozorious and Yippie were piled on Lucille's lap along with a big bouquet of roses. I was guessing they were for me.

After intermission, the backdrop containing the pond scene came rolling down and the big rock and wispy willow tree were wheeled out onto the stage. When the curtain opened again I was wearing my sparkly mermaid costume and acting bored.

We were finally at the point in the story where I'd left off with Lucille. I knew she was eager to find out what happened next.

I sat at the water's edge in my mermaid costume and sighed as the narrator spoke: "Iris eventually realized that lounging around all day and doing nothing except for playing the flute occasionally* got pretty boring, *pretty* fast. Although she pitied the fish in the pond because they were all exactly the same, swimming here and there, with not so much as a care, she also secretly found herself wishing that she could go back to being just another girl in a village. And she realized that being just another fish in a pond or girl in a village wasn't such a bad thing after all."

Suddenly Liam, in his role as a fish, popped his head out from behind the rock. I acted startled by him.

"Why do you pity me so?" he asked.

"I don't pity you," I replied.

80

But the fish argued, "I'm a fish with special powers. I can read your thoughts and I know for a fact that you pity me."

I confessed as I sang to the fish:

I feel sorry for you because, except for your names, you all appear to be just the same—with no individuality*—it's really a shame.

Then the wise fish replied in song:

It's true. In many ways we are just the same. But we're also different in more ways than just our name. We may appear to swim about, aimlessly. But, look much closer, what do you see?

I leaned closer to the fish. "I see a twinkle in your eyes. And I see the colors of the rainbow reflecting off your orange scales."

Exactly, sang the fish. *From a distance, my scales may look like all the others but they are different, in fact. We're all quite different—the fish in my pack. My eyes have their own special twinkle and my thoughts are my own. My scales are unique with their rainbow-like tone.*

"I see," I said.

The fish spoke. "We're all born with our own special gifts. For instance, I can read minds. None of the other fish in the pond can do that. Another fish, named Cleo, is the fastest swimmer in the pond, and then there's Hector. He can jump out of the water and do a triple flip in the air."

Liam stood up and called out to the audience. "Treasure those things you have in common and appreciate your differences!" Then he raised his hands over his head and pretended to dive back into the pond and swim away.

The audience clapped.

I sat back down on the rock, put my hand on my chin and sighed again. Then suddenly, the frog reappeared.

"Please," I begged the frog, "I no longer wish to be a mermaid. Turn me back into a young girl."

The frog sang:

But I'm just a frog, sitting here on this log. My powers are limited as such—so as not to benefit you— very much!

I threw myself onto the fake rock and pretended to be sobbing.

The curtain closed. I knew this was one of my fastest costume changes and we all had to work together to get it done quickly and right.

The rest of the crew members swapped out the set while Ali and Darlene whisked me over to one of the stage wings and helped me remove my mermaid costume. I had worn a tank top and shorts underneath so that I wouldn't have to waste time going all the way back to my dressing room to change. Darlene helped me into my kimono while Ali styled my hair back into a high bun and added the hair sticks.

Meanwhile, the backdrop containing the garden scene flew down from the rafters* and the large green contraption that Kiley had made was wheeled out onto the stage.

In less than a minute, the set was transformed back into a garden and I was onstage, lying on a bench, as though fast asleep. A boy named Eric, playing the grandfather, shook me gently.

"Wake up Iris. You're having a bad dream."

I stood up and pretended to be elated that I was once again a young village girl.

The narrator spoke: "Iris awoke from her dream and suddenly saw things in a whole new light. She realized that looking and acting the same as all the other village girls didn't mean that she wasn't unique. And she noticed things that she hadn't given much thought to before. For example, each of the tiny petals on the blooming crocus flowers had their own individual design. And when she gazed over at the pond she no longer saw a bunch of fish swimming about aimlessly. She saw a fish that had shiny rainbow-colored scales and the ability to read minds, and another that could do a triple flip in the air."

The narrator continued: "Tiny buds were now beginning to form on the orchid plant. Iris recognized this as a sign of new beginnings and a fresh outlook on life. She realized that some differences are small, while others are great, but each and every one of us possesses our own special trait.*"

I threw my arms around the grandfather and promised that in the future I'd show more respect for his flowers and all living things. Then I sang the final words from the song, "Being Me":

Grateful for tutoring, grateful for tea, grateful for being just plain old me!

At the end, the entire audience stood up and applauded. The curtain closed and all the cast and crew members converged* onto the stage.

When the curtain reopened we all took turns taking our bows.

I was the last one to bow. As I walked to the front of the stage I could hear people whistling and shouting my name. Lucille ran up to the front of the stage and held out the pretty bouquet of roses. I leaned over and accepted them from her.

I could tell by the look on her face that she was oh so very proud of me.

Chapter Ten

BEING ME

After the performance, my mom and dad snapped a few photos of Kiley and me. Then Kiley came back to my dressing room and waited while I changed. The school was hosting a cast party in the cafeteria for all the drama club students and their families. Kiley and I told our parents that we'd meet them there.

Kiley chose to stay in her all-black crew outfit because that's just who she was. And I changed into a pretty pink party dress because that's just who *I* was!

The hallway was buzzing with activity and excitement. Families posed for pictures while other kids hurried down the hallway toward the cafeteria.

As Kiley and I made our way to the cafeteria we

noticed Liam walking toward us. He was easy to spot because he was still wearing his fish head costume. But now he had a bright red scarf tied around his neck.

"Here. That guy that's been hanging around, talking to Mr. D for the past few months—he said his name was Mr. Rose, I think. He asked me to give you guys these." Liam handed us both two flat, square, wrapped packages.

"What are they?" I asked.

"I don't know. I'm just the delivery boy," said Liam. "He said he had to leave. That guy's pretty cool though. I told him I liked his scarf and he took it off and gave it to me. See?" Liam extended his chin out of his fish costume and attempted to look downward at the bright red scarf.

"Yes, Liam. We see," smirked Kiley.

"Well, go ahead and open them. I want to see what he gave you guys," Liam commanded.

There was a card attached to mine. I opened it and read it out loud: "To a very special star. Keep up the good work! Regards, Mr. Rose."

Then Kiley read her card: "To a talented and creative young lady. You remind me of myself when I was younger. Best Wishes, Mr. Rose."

"I'm waiting," Liam said impatiently.

Kiley and I tore into the wrapping paper. Inside were copies of the script from the play, bound in hardcover with fancy gold writing on the front that read: *Once Upon an Elf. Written by Albert A. Rose.* I re-read the "written by" part.

"Did Mr. Rose write this play?" I asked.

"I don't know," Kiley replied.

"That would explain why he spent so much time at our rehearsals," Liam said.

Then Liam pulled out his camera and asked a passerby to snap a picture of the three of us. Kiley and I held up our scripts while Liam made one of his many strange faces.

As the camera flash went off, Liam turned his head sideways so that only one side of his face was visible inside the goldfish head. "Look!" he exclaimed. "There he is. Over there near the exit!"

Mr. Rose was shaking another adult's hand as he stepped toward the doorway. The three of us scrambled toward him.

"Mr. Rose!" I called out as we weaved through the crowd of people.

Mr. Rose turned but couldn't see us because we were surrounded by so many adults who were much taller than us.

Liam called over to him again. "Mr. Rose! Wait

up!" And thanks to Liam's oversized fish costume, he was able to figure out that there was a fish head and possibly a few other kids headed his way.

We quickly caught up to Mr. Rose and thanked him for the gifts.

"Did you really write this?" Kiley asked.

"I did—a long time ago. I wasn't much of an actor. I was more of a behind-the-scenes person, like you," he said to her. "But I loved the theater so I got involved by working with the crew and then I eventually took up writing. Soon after, I followed my passion to Broadway* and New York City where I wrote this play. It was a big hit back in the day."

"And I have to say," he continued, "you certainly did justice* to it. It's great to see a group of nice young kids doing such a professional job."

"Thanks!" I said.

"This gift means a lot to us," said Kiley. She thanked him as well.

We both knew it was something we'd treasure forever.

"Well, it's late, and I'm a bit tired, so I'm going home now," said Mr. Rose. "You guys have fun at the cast party."

"We will," said Liam as he nodded his big fish head up and down.

"By the way, that scarf looks good on you," said Mr. Rose, chuckling at the sight of him.

"Although I was never meant for the limelight," he addressed all three of us, "I still liked to wear a little something now and again that made a statement. It was my way of expressing my individuality. When you all get a little older, you'll have more freedom to do that, too."

I smiled, knowing he was right. Then we all said our goodbyes.

As Kiley, Liam and I made our way over to the cast party I thought about what Mr. Rose had said. It was true. I had plenty of time to figure out who I was and express my uniqueness.

But for now, I was *sorta kinda* looking forward to going back to being just another girl in a school full of kids—another star on a door or a fish in the sea—just *me*!

Glossary

Many words have more than one meaning. Here are the definitions of words marked with this symbol * (an asterisk) as they are used in sentences.

accordion: *a portable musical instrument with large folds or bellows that push air through to make music*

aimlessly: *without direction or purpose*

Broadway: *the main theater district in New York City*

choreographer: *a person who creates and teaches dance moves and steps*

cold, as in "down cold": *having something memorized or knowing it well*

commotion: *a lot of noise, activity*

compose: *to calm yourself*

contraption: *a gadget or device*

contributing: *adding to or playing a part in*

converged: *came together as a group*

cue: *a signal, during a play, that reminds an actor or crew member to do a particular thing*

dolly: *a platform with wheels used for moving something large or heavy*

domain: *area or territory*

established: *figured out*

filaments: *thin, stem-like parts of a flower extending from its center*

flawless: *perfect, just right*

hemline: *the bottom edge of a skirt or garment*

individuality: *what makes one person different from others*

introductory: *beginning*

justice, as in "did justice to it": *showed or presented something in a good way*

kimono: *a traditional Japanese robe*

limelight, as in "in the limelight": *being the center of attention, usually on stage and under a spotlight*

mangled: *ruined*

marveling: *admiring, being amazed by*

narrator: *speaker, storyteller*

nurtured: *looked after, cared for*

occasionally: *once in awhile*

passionate: *having strong, loving feelings for something*

perspective: *point of view*

pod: *part of a plant that contains seeds*

pollination: *the process by which pollen is transported from one flower to another to produce seeds*

porcelain: *a type of china normally used in dishware*

predicament: *a difficult situation*

professional: *done with a high level of skill, for pay*

prop list: *a list of items to be used onstage during a play*

proposition: *an offer or suggestion*

rafters: *beams that support a roof (in a theater, backdrops may be attached to them)*

reside: *live or exist in*

rifled (rifle): *searched through*

script: *the written words of a play*

solo: *a song sung by only one person*

spacious: *large, roomy*

spectacle: *something that is odd or unusual looking*

stage wings: *the sides of the stage not seen by the audience*

thrive: *grow, bloom or become healthy*

tidal wave: *an unusually large wave or movement of water*

trait: *a special quality that makes a person different*

wing, as in "drama wing": *an addition to or extension of a building*

wiser, as in "no one was the wiser": *no one knew what had happened*

How to Make a Tissue Paper Flower

You can make flowers just like Evelyn and Kiley did in the story. Here's how:

What You'll Need:

Pipe cleaners
Tissue paper
Ruler
Scissors

1. Cut paper into rectangles (6" x 8" or preferred size).
2. Stack 4 or 5 pieces together.
3. Pleat and fold paper like an accordion.
4. If desired, tear corners of the tissue paper for a more natural look.
5. Take one end of the pipe cleaner, wrap it around the center of the folded paper, then twist it tight.
6. Fluff out the folds and separate each of the layers to form a pretty flower.

*Remember, craft projects should always
be supervised by your parent or a trusted adult.
Small items should be kept away from
smaller children at all times.*

12 Tips for Auditioning for a Play

1. Know the play or musical you're auditioning for
If there is a movie about the play, watch it.
If there is a script, read it.

2. Find out what's required of you for the audition
Are you expected to read lines, sing a song or dance?

3. Choose the role you want and learn all you can about the character
A movie or online production can help you to get into character.

4. Know your lines
Study your lines and have them down cold.

5. Practice your dance steps
Practicing—over and over again—makes it perfect!

6. If you're required to sing, rehearse your solo
Downloading music can help you.
Practicing in front of a mirror can also help.

7. Dress appropriately
On the day of the audition, do not wear clothing that's too flashy or distracting.

8. Be punctual
Being tardy is not a good way to begin an audition. On the day of the audition, double-check driving directions and be sure to arrive on time.

9. Walk onto the stage with confidence and with your head held high

Good posture and confidence can go a long way in an audition.

10. Be sure to project (speak loudly) when you speak your lines and sing your solo

Directors will want to make sure that audience members can hear and understand you from the stage.

11. If you're allowed to read from a script, hold it away from your face so that people in the audience can see you

12. Last, but not least, have a positive attitude and try to do your best!

Remember, always ask a parent or trusted adult for help with downloading/viewing movies and music.

About the Author

Julie Driscoll keeps a notebook with her at all times because everywhere she goes, something funny or exciting happens that she knows would make for an interesting story.

Her greatest inspirations are her two daughters, Emily and Kerry, and her husband, Steve, who's a lot like a little kid trapped inside a grown-up's body.

Mrs. Driscoll is a writer and artist. She has written a screenplay in the family genre and a television pilot for a local network.

*In addition to **In the Limelight**, Mrs. Driscoll has written four other books in the Our Generation® Series, **The Jumpstart Squad**, **Adventures at Shelby Stables**, **The Note in the Piano** and **Blizzard on Moose Mountain**.*

this is **my** audition story:

_____

_____

_____

_____

_____

_____

_____

_____

_____

_____

_____

_____